The Jewel and Her Lapidary

The jewel and her lapidary

F

Wilde, Fran

DATE DUE

ALSO BY FRAN WILDE

Updraft
Cloudbound (forthcoming)

THE JEWEL
AND HER
LAPIDARY

FRAN WILDE

A TOM DOHERTY ASSOCIATES BOOK

NEW YORK

THE JEWEL AND HER LAPIDARY

Copyright © 2016 by Fran Wilde

Cover art by Tommy Arnold
Cover designed by Christine Foltzer

Edited by Patrick Nielsen Hayden

A Tor.com Book
Published by Tom Doherty Associates, LLC
175 Fifth Avenue
New York, NY 10010

www.tor.com

Tor® is a registered trademark of Tom Doherty Associates, LLC.

ISBN 978-0-7653-8497-3 (ebook)
ISBN 978-0-7653-8983-1 (trade paperback)

First Edition: May 2016

For Susan

The Jewel and Her Lapidary

Visitors to the Jeweled Valley should expect rustic accommodations and varying degrees of adventure, as the area is both remote and not under protection of any State or Commonwealth.

There are two inns of varying reputation (p. 34) and attractive scenery, including walks to the Ruins (p. 30), the Variegated Riverbank (p. 29), and the stone formation colloquially known as the Jewel and Her Lapidary (p. 32).

The best place to find a guide is at the Deaf King, a tavern by the river (p. 33).

Local guides can become verbose on matters of history and legend. Indeed, some cannot discern between the two. Many locals will gladly inform you their forebears served at the Jeweled Court long ago. More than a few will declare their ancestors were Jewels—royalty who wore the region's ancient gems—or their assistants. This is likely untrue, as the last Jewels were murdered in a palace coup after six generations of peaceful rule.

. . . from **A Guide to the Remote River**
Valleys, *by **M. Lankin, East Quadril***

~

Strips of soft cloth bound the Jewel Lin's hands behind her back, knotted as if they'd been tied in a hurry. When her head cleared enough for her to think of it, Lin slid her hands back and forth until the bindings loosened and she was able to bend her wrists and tug at the ties.

Her mouth felt dry as a stone. Her legs and feet tingled, as if she'd been sitting on them for hours at a strange angle. *Sima,* she thought. *Where is Sima?* Lin could not see anything. *What happened?* Sima would know. Or Aba.

An elbow pressed Lin's side in the darkness. Lin heard her lapidary grunt and wriggle, trying to release herself. Sima's kicking dislodged something heavy and dry that rattled like bones across the floor.

When Lin had freed her hands, she touched the cloth that covered her eyes and ears, then pulled at that knot too. The blindfold fell into her hands. It was strips from the veil Lin had worn since she was eleven.

On the rough ground nearby, the ancient bone Sima had kicked stared at them: a skull turned to opal, eye sockets stuffed with raw yellow topaz.

Lin knew where they were now. Far from her private quarters, where they'd drunk their evening tea and gone to sleep. They were below the moonstone hall, in the pit beside the throne. Where Aba had always threatened to put her as a child when she misbehaved.

Lin bit down on her fist, stifling a scream. She looked around the pit, expecting to see the rest of the Jeweled Court similarly bound. Light flickered through the grate above her head. Sima still wriggled beside her in the dark. But beyond Sima, she saw nothing but darkness and more ancient bones.

She reached for her lapidary's hands. She felt the cloth that bound them and discovered that it had been looped around the metal cuffs and chains that marked Sima not just as a gem-speaker but as a lapidary—Lin's own lapidary: the bound courtier to a royal Jewel. Sima had been blindfolded too, with cloth ripped from her blue lapidary's cloak. She'd been gagged as well.

Lin worked at the knots. *We have been betrayed. The court. The valley.*

No one else sat in the pit with them. Above, the muffled sounds grew louder. Lin heard running feet. Shouting. Someone howled.

Lin wanted to stuff her hand back in her mouth. She wanted to go back to her room and see her father in the morning. To tell him about her nightmare. Lights flickered through the grate over her head.

"No," Sima whimpered, panic edging her voice. "A lapidary must not—" She was looking up, through the grate. She had not addressed her words to Lin.

Must not do what? thought Lin. *Which lapidary?* Her thoughts were slow and muddled. *The tea must have been drugged.* What had happened to her family? They had ordered wine in the hall while they discussed matters of state, and she'd been told to retire.

Above them, a voice shouted, "Shattered! We are shattered. You should have listened to me!"

The voice was barely recognizable as belonging to the King's Lapidary. Sima's father.

"Stop," Sima begged, climbing to her feet. Tears ran down her cheeks, turning diamond in the moonlight. She put a hand against the wall to steady herself. "Let us out, let us help you. Father." Her last word was a wail.

The screams continued above their heads, wave after crashing wave of them.

Father. Lin called out, "Help us!" She shouted for the king while Sima called to the lapidary. Two daughters below. Two fathers above.

Sima looked at Lin with wide eyes. "He is gem-mad."

The King's Lapidary howled in answer. His words came faster and faster, tumbling through the grate. Their meaning was nearly drowned by his laughter. Lin caught her name. She heard "bargain" and "promise." The lapidary's voice rose to a high pitch and cracked.

Sharp metal struck stone. Sima grabbed her ears, holding tight to the metal bands that wrapped her earlobes. Through clenched teeth, she whispered, "A lapidary must obey their Jewel." The first vow a new lapidary took. Sima repeated the vow like a chant as a shriek pierced the room above them. Her face was white, but she pushed Lin away from the grate, whispering, "He's going to break the diamond; he'll break it and death will come. Cover your ears!"

When the stone shattered it made a noise like a mineshaft collapsing, and a scream, and a fire all at once. Sima's eyes rolled back and Lin scrambled to keep her courtier's head from hitting the hard pit walls. "It's all right," she whispered. Nothing was right. Where was her father? Where were her sisters and brothers? And their lapidaries?

The pit and its metal walls seemed to protect them from the gems, and from Sima's father. Above, a cry of pain reverberated through the hall. Then something like rain. Then weeping. She heard the clatter as the palace guard dropped their weapons en masse and tried to flee, feet pounding, across the great hall's moonstone tiles. She heard them fall, one by one.

Metal struck again. Sima threw up at Lin's feet.

"Father!" Lin shouted, hoping her voice would pass up through the grate. "What is happening?"

Instead of the king, the lapidary returned to kneel on the grate. His hands gripped the bars, charred black. His eyes looked bloodred in the moonlight. "Awake," he muttered. "Awake too soon. The commander has not yet come and you must cover your ears. You will be no good to me mad." His voice singsonged as he stood and laughed, then lurched away.

"Sima," Lin whispered. "What is he doing?"

Her lapidary whimpered. "He is breaking his vows, my Jewel. He has broken gems. Couldn't you hear? The Opaque Sapphire. The Death Astrion. The Steadfast Diamond. He is about to break the Star Cabochon. We have to stop him."

The Opaque Sapphire. The Jeweled Palace was visible to attackers without that gem. And she and Sima were trapped in the pit beside the throne. The astrion and the diamond. The borders were undefended.

All her life, Aba had made Lin recite the valley's legends. How the first gems had enslaved those who found them; how they had maddened those who could hear them. How the first Jewel, the Deaf King, had set a cabochon-cut ruby with metal and wire. How he'd bound those who heard the stones as well and named them lapidaries. Made them serve him instead of the gems. How the gems had protected the valley better than any army.

She'd made Lin learn what could happen if a lapidary broke their vows.

The screaming had quieted above them. Sima knelt and cupped her hands so that Lin could stand on them. Lin pressed on the grate with both hands. The heavy door lifted an inch, but little more. Lin climbed to Sima's shoulders.

"Here—" Sima handed Lin a long bone from the pit floor. They wedged the grate open and Lin pulled herself out. Looking around, she could not see the King's Lapidary. But as Sima pulled herself up using a stretch of Lin's robe, Lin saw her own father, lying on the ground. His eyes were clouded like ruined opals. His breath bubbled in the blood-flecked foam at his mouth. An amber goblet rolled on the floor near his fingers. The bodies of the rest of the court lay scattered. Sisters. Brothers. Aba. Lin bound her heart up with the words. Saw their lips too: blackened and covered with foam. Poison.

Sima crossed the hall, following a sound. A voice. In the courtyard beyond the throne, the King's Lapidary stood on the high wall. He pointed at Lin, before Sima moved to stand between them. "The Western Mountains are coming—I've promised them a powerful gem and one very fine Jewel to marry!" He began to laugh and shout again. "They are strong! Our gems are fading. Soon their only power will be to catch the eye. The Jeweled Valley *must* be protected. He wouldn't listen. I protected you!"

Lapidaries' lathes were smashed across the courtyard. Shards of the Intaglio Amethyst that mapped the valley's mines crunched under Sima's feet as she walked toward her father.

"You cannot betray your vows, Father. You promised."

Metal rained down on them as the gem-mad lapidary threw the chains and bracelets that had bound his arms and ears. "No longer!"

Sima sank to her knees in the courtyard and Lin fell beside her. They watched as the madman waited for his conquering army on the wall.

Then the King's Lapidary fell quiet for the first time since Lin woke.

The two girls listened, shaking in the cold, for the mountain army's drums. They wondered how long the palace's doors could hold. But no drums came. Only silence. The King's Lapidary climbed up on the lip of the palace wall. He turned to face the courtyard. His lips were pressed tight, his eyes rolled. He spread his arms wide. His hands clutched at the air.

Sima rose to her feet. Began to run toward the wall.

Without another word, the King's Lapidary leapt from the wall, his blue robe flapping, the chains on his wrists and ankles ringing in the air.

And before Lin could scream, the King's Lapidary crashed to the flagstones of the courtyard.

When Lin came to her senses, Sima was whispering to her sapphires and blue topaz, the ones that lined her veil. *Calm,* she whispered. *Calm.*

The valley's gems. In a gem-speaker's hands, Lin knew they amplified desire. When bezel-set and held by a trained lapidary, they had to obey: to protect, calm, compel. Only without their bezels, or in the presence of a wild gem-speaker or a gem-mad lapidary, could gems do worse things.

Sima's gems did calm Lin. She remained aware of what was happening, but they were smooth facets made out of fact; her terror was trapped within. She was the only one left. An army was coming. The court of the Jeweled Valley—which had known peace for four hundred years, since the Deaf King set the Star Cabochon—had been betrayed. Lin felt a keen rising in her chest.

"Make me stronger," she ordered Sima.

Sima tried her best. She whispered to the small topaz and diamonds at Lin's wrists and ears. Lin could not hear the gems, but she felt them acting on her. Compelling her to be calm. To think clearly. She took a breath. Stood.

"We will collect all the gems we can find, Sima," she said. "All the chain mail too."

They searched the bodies of the court for gems. Lin sewed the gems herself into one of her old gray cloaks.

When she rolled her eldest brother's body on its side to peel the ornamental chain mail from his chest, she wept, but it was a calm, slow weeping. The gems allowed her time to act. She would have to mourn later. She moved from one body to the next. Sima followed behind, tugging cloaks, searching pockets.

Sima removed the bands and chains from the fallen lapidaries, cutting the solder points with her father's diamond saw.

They returned to Lin's quarters in the heart of the palace and Lin wrapped herself in all of the chains she had collected. She pointed to the metal bands, the oaths meaningless now.

"You must do the rest," she told her lapidary.

Sima, whispering her vows, shook her head. "I cannot do this work, my Jewel. It will harm you."

The small betrayal made the lapidary wince.

"Sima, you must." Lin spoke calmly, and Sima pulled the cache of tools from her sleeve. She lit her torch. Attached bands at Lin's wrists and ankles. The metal grew hot. Lin felt her skin burn and thought of her sisters and brothers. Blisters rose where Sima's torch came too close.

Lin ached for her father.

"The mountains wish a bride and a throne," Lin said. Her voice was flat. Her new veil hung heavy against her temples.

Sima added more chains to Lin's veil. When Lin demanded it, she spoke the binding verses she'd learned at her own father's side.

And then Sima backed out the door, latching it behind her. Lin listened to the lapidary's metal vows clattering and chiming on her arms as she sped away. *To the river, Sima. Run.*

The noises faded. The palace of the Jeweled Court fell silent.

And Lin, for the first time in her life, was completely alone.

~

In her second act of betrayal, Sima gritted her teeth and began to remove the metal vows that bound her from wrists to biceps. They would make too much noise as she ran.

She cut away the engraved silver chains with her father's diamond saw, then started on the bands. The metal was too noisy and would give her away. When the saw broke, the last lapidary of the Jeweled Valley twisted and bent the bands, thinking, *Hurry, please hurry,* until the first of them—*A lapidary protects the valley*—snapped from metal fatigue.

Her father's body lay broken in the outer courtyard. Sima pushed the image of his fall from her memory; blocked the sound his bones had made on the flagstones from her ears. There was no time to mourn the King's Lapidary, no time to consider his treachery. *Hurry.* She beat back the last moments of the court—seven royal Jewels choking from poison, the palace guard run away, six lapidaries dead. Her father's doing.

Traitor, the gems hidden in Sima's stolen cloak echoed her thought. They magnified the word so it almost enveloped her. The gems spoke louder now that she'd broken several vows of her own. Louder, too, because her father had broken all of his.

Sima knew she was not yet a traitor. She'd kept her most important vows—the platinum bands that wrapped the lobes of her ears and made no noise—hoping she might avoid her father's fate. *A lapidary protects their Jewel,* said one. *A lapidary protects the gems in their care,* said the other. Those vows would not make noise as she fled. They would keep her safe and sane, she hoped.

When the last armband snapped and the words engraved upon it fell away, she wrapped the metal with torn, bloody cloth. She tucked the cloth in the pocket she'd hung from her belt.

The metal, together with the lesser gems of the valley already sewn into her cloak's hem, weighed heavy but made no sound save for the gems' whispers.

Sima tried to ignore those.

She ran for the far palace wall and prepared to leave her fallen kingdom and its last Jewel—the princess Lin—behind.

The army from the Western Mountains was already entering the valley. It would soon take the palace. Its soldiers would expect to find her father at the gates, welcoming them. But the King's Lapidary had climbed the very steps Sima now climbed.

At the place where her father had jumped to his death, Sima threw a rope over the embrasure.

The valley was the most important thing now. She had to get herself and the gems away from the valley. It was what Lin wanted. If Sima stayed, and the army caught her, they would use both gems and lapidary against the people of the valley.

She wrapped her newly bare hands around the rough fiber, took a breath, and asked the gems for strength. Then she stepped over the palace wall, into choking smoke from the fires that already ringed the valley. Her cloak caught the hot wind and tugged her backward, causing her to clutch the rope, finally afraid.

The hidden gems—rough-cut emeralds; opals and topaz; lesser sapphires; one ruby, but not the biggest one—whispered muffled and useless things. *Survival. Escape. Betrayal.*

"Quiet," she whispered back. Her voice cracked. She looked over her shoulder to the dark ground below, then across the open field to the trees and the hidden caves by the river. If she could get there, she might fulfill one vow, even as another weakened close to breaking.

The gems did not listen to her. The whispers continued, until they were drowned beneath a new sound.

The beat of heavy drums echoed through the valley as the army of the Western Mountains advanced unchallenged. Sima heard cries rise sharp and high as ironclad soldiers woke the cottages. Artisans and miners begged for their lives and those of their families. Sima's left foot slipped on the ash-slick wall, then found a place to brace. The weighted cloak pulled at her. The army closed on the palace gates and began to pound at them. When Sima moved again, her right foot slipped. Her shoes were meant for smooth palace floors, not rough walls. She forced herself to lean back against the rope, to press her feet firmly, and to move faster. She tried to forget how high she was and what a fall did to a body. Tried to forget the soldiers now assaulting the palace's inner gates.

She marked her escape in the rough increments of rope and wall. In broken bands, broken vows, broken gems.

Not so long ago, the palace would have been hidden to its enemies, thanks to the Opaque Sapphire. The Death Astrion, the Steadfast Diamond, and the Star Cabochon would have held the borders and repelled the army. No longer.

A lapidary who betrays their Jewel will be shattered. The second band she'd cut from her wrist. The one her father had soldered for the first time when she was three years old, on the day of the Jewel Lin's birth. Sima sucked a breath at remembered pain and at the rope's harsh burn, both. She'd been at Lin's side every day since. Slept on a pallet by her bed, made her beautiful baubles. She'd been there when her father had drugged their tea, then thrown them bound and gagged into the silver-lined pit below the throne. She had failed to protect her Jewel.

No. She'd also been there to make Lin cover her ears as the rest of the court died. As the gems shattered.

Sima inched closer to the ground as the pounding continued. She heard the muffled sounds of inlaid doors crying out against the iron battering ram: *Strength. Fortitude.*

Those doors would hold until their last gem broke. When it did, the palace would fall with Lin inside, bound head to toe in platinum chains.

Sima's feet touched the ground. She gathered the edges of her heavy cloak around her and turned toward the trees. Rough stones tore her soft shoes. Her feet sank deep into mud, but she kept running. If she could make the river, the boatman could smuggle her away and both gems and lapidary would pass out of reach. She would no longer endanger the valley.

The gems whispered, tried to tempt her with power and freedom. They'd done the same when she was a child, before she'd been bound. With every step farther from Lin, the gems grew louder.

The King's Lapidary, broken by his treachery, had freed the oldest gem among them: the cabochon star ruby, called the Star Cabochon. Now the minor gems clamored for control from within her cloak. Coronation sapphires, topaz, Lin's birth emeralds. Gems to ease pain, to give courage, if they were bound correctly. Without a proper setting, each could wreak havoc on the valley. For those who could hear them, more bindings were required as protection. Vows.

"A lapidary obeys her Jewel," Sima whispered, her voice shaking. "A lapidary guards her gems." She fought to hold her vows in her mind. The gems quieted for the moment. But every lapidary learned early that even the strongest among them had a breaking point.

And Sima knew she was not very strong. She'd been nowhere near as strong as her father. And he'd shattered.

She would not break her promises to Lin. She would keep going.

Lapidaries must know the number of gems in their possession, their settings, their powers. The long vow made her wheeze to say it while she ran. That had been a spiral cuff, the easiest to remove.

Escape, whispered the gems in the smoke and shadows. *Release.* Sima kept running. She had to hold out long enough to get in a boat. Iron hated deep water. The river was the only way out, though no gem protected the woods. Not anymore.

Oh, Lin, Sima thought, and almost turned around. The lapidaries' vows broken. The valley endangered once again by its gems. The legend had turned real. Now she was the last lapidary. Now she had become a thief. Now the last Jewel sat chained in her palace, her people betrayed.

The mud of the forest turned to sand and grit beneath Sima's feet. She was close to the river now. She crouched low, kneeling in the shadows. She could see the water glint through the last trees. No soldiers patrolled the riverbank. She tried to catch her breath.

If she had been strong enough to destroy the minor gems herself, she'd still be at Lin's side. But they had both spent years living with the gems. If the wrong gem broke, their minds would shatter, like Sima's father's. The Western Mountains' army would claim the rest of the gems. And even a mad lapidary could cut stones, if properly bound.

Sima had to leave. She knew that. Even as it broke her.

"I'll scatter them to every corner of the six kingdoms, Lin," Sima whispered again. "I promise. I won't return."

A lapidary obeys her Jewel. She would keep that vow. She stepped from the shadows and toward the river, pulling her hood up over her head. She bent her shoulders and prepared to run again.

A shout broke the night behind her. A thick iron gauntlet wrapped her arm. Spun her around.

A plumed iron helm loomed over Sima, dark against the night sky. The soldier cuffed her hard with his other hand, then tossed her over his shoulder. Her vision swam. Her ears rang. Gems whispered, *Weakness. Failure.* The hem of the cloak dragged heavy through the valley's ashes all the way back to the palace's broken gates.

~

The only way to be comfortable beneath her veil of chains, Lin discovered, was to kneel on the moonstone floor with Sima's blue cloak beneath her knees for padding.

She passed her final minutes of freedom thinking of her father's profile, his ready smile. She pushed aside her last vision of him, his face purple, the choking noises deep in his throat. Replaced that with memories of him on the amber throne, greeting his subjects. She loved that he'd liked to meet their gaze. Said often that he could tell a true valleyman by the way they looked you in the eye.

Father. In the waiting silence of the palace, Lin pressed her fists hard against floor and chain. Felt the pain that bloomed there.

Days earlier, Lin's gauze betrothal veil had hung beneath her crown, making her father's face, and those of her brothers and the court, soft in the light. Set in her eleventh year, when she'd been promised to a young prince of the Eastern Seas, the soft veil would not be lifted until she married. In private quarters, she'd peeked from beneath the cloth. She'd studied the way time sat heavy below her father's eyes when he consulted his lapidary. When he thought she did not see him.

Now her father was gone, and Lin had replaced the soft veil with one made of platinum chain.

If she'd been a proper Jewel, one trained to command powerful lapidaries, to rule a kingdom, she felt she might have come up with a better plan than this. But the commander of the Western Mountains demanded her as bride, sought to gain her throne as well as the valley's major gems. Lin was determined to slow their plans at least, in her father's memory. If Lin could get away, perhaps help would come—perhaps from the Eastern Seas—given time.

The door to the great hall and the royal quarters shouted and cracked. Another stone shattered.

A Jewel does not cry. She does not frown. Lin's Aba said this long ago while pinching her arm. *Your kingdom is your setting, you are its light.*

Though her Aba would never instruct anyone again, Lin wished now for her guidance, even the kind that pinched her to be quiet, the kind that ignored her questions. She had such doubts, such fears.

What was a Jewel without a lapidary? Without a court? Without a kingdom? Lin traced a finger down the fine mail chains. How did one lead a kingdom? She'd never thought to ask before.

Lin knew her eyes were dry and clear, her face still. These were the facets of herself she had been taught to control.

The part of her that was still afraid listened to the palace doors resist the mountain army. That part jumped with each slam of iron against wood and gold and gem. That part had seen her father dying, breath bubbling foam, lips black with poison.

The doors shattered with a great cry, the gems—a rosette of rubies and diamonds cut in steadfast patterns—falling broken from their settings. She could not often hear gemstones, but this cry was so loud, every member of the palace left alive could hear.

Which meant Lin was the only one who heard: *Despair. Surrender.*

Running feet in heavy armor crossed the palace's moonstone tiles. Yells echoed down hallways, punctuated by the sound of more breaking doors. Then Lin's door smashed open. Two soldiers entered, bragging loudly about mysterious gems and riches, about honor.

When they saw Lin kneeling beneath her veil, they fell silent. They stared.

What do you see? Lin wondered as she rose. *A Jewel? A girl?* She planted her feet shoulder width apart, as far as the chains would allow. Sima had left her a few ways to defend herself, if they got close enough.

One soldier advanced, his armor creaking. "Don't cause us any trouble. Commander Nal wants you well."

Lin waited and the soldier stepped forward again. He reached a hand out to her, keeping his other hand on his sword, well back from her reach.

She spoke then. "You will let me walk on my own. I am a Jewel of the valley."

The two men laughed. "You *were* a Jewel. Where are

your gems?"

The first soldier caught hold of Lin's left wrist. She snapped a chain hard between his gauntlet and his arm guard. Dragged hard on it with all her weight, until the man cried out. "Little witch!"

He disentangled himself, but not before she looped another chain around his sword hilt, dangling from his left hand, and had it almost immobilized. She reached for it with her right hand, fingertips straining, but her own chains held her back. The soldier snapped her around, chain mail ringing, into the wall.

"I told you to behave."

Her head banged against chains and stone. Her ears rang with impact, but she stayed on her feet. She'd never been struck so hard before. Sima had practiced fighting with her, as had her brothers until she'd been betrothed, but none ever hit her like this.

Lin felt the lack of her gems then more than ever. For her pain, Sima would have whispered peace to the opals. The gems in their settings would have magnified the feeling, eased her pain. Sapphires, spoken properly, would have radiated calm.

Instead, Lin had nothing to cushion the blow but despair and loss.

She let go of the sword's hilt. Stopped trying to tangle the clumsy soldiers in her chains. Beneath her veil, sweat ran into her eyes and made them sting. Her hair caught in the chains and tangled painfully when she turned her head. She tasted iron in her mouth.

The soldier waited until she knelt. Then he secured her hands behind her.

A Jewel holds her head up, Aba might have said. *She leads by example.*

Except that Aba had never spoken to her of leadership. No one had. Her father, brothers, and sisters had kept much from her. Because she was so young. *Our one perfect Jewel,* they'd said, and shooed her from the room when the lapidaries conferred and the diplomats debated. She and Sima too.

She'd always demanded to stay, but Aba had started in with the *musts* and the *does nots.* Sima had gently steered her from anything remotely like harm. She'd been ordered to care for Lin like any treasure being readied for export.

But when Aba napped, Lin had demanded her lapidary join her to listen at doorways and bribe the maids who waited at table. She'd gathered as much gossip as she could. She'd learned about the kingdoms and what they sold. She'd strained to hear the stories of newfound gems and their risks and powers.

Gossip and heavy doors blurred sound as much as her gauze veil had blurred sight. Lin had seen nothing of the kingdom clearly and she knew it.

The soldier leaned in once to lift Lin to his shoulder. He couldn't figure out how to put his hands on her without becoming tangled in her chains. Lin, her head throbbing, refused to help him. Fear overwhelmed her. Memories broke loose. She had no gems to calm her. To keep her from shaking as the soldier lifted her to take her to meet the commander. A new betrothal.

Betrayal. Betrothal. She imagined the lapidary's hands on her father's goblet, as soldiers grabbed at her chains. Father drank his final wine and the great gems shattered. *Strangers in the palace. No one coming to help.* Those who hadn't gone mad from gems or died from poison had run away. But Lin would not run. She would face her fate. She stopped shaking.

Because a Jewel protects their people. It was what her father would have done.

Were there people left to protect? The artisans and miners, the craftsmen, and the people of the valley still lived.

Perhaps the mountain army would relent, once they realized the gems were broken and no Lapidaries remained to speak the gems. Perhaps Lin could stall long enough to negotiate terms that would help her people. She hoped to try.

The soldier released her bound hands and jerked her arms up as high as they would go. The chains rattled. He hauled her forward and bent his shoulder.

Her chains hit his armor like hail on a rooftop, sharp and slick and cold.

Without a word, the soldier turned and carried Lin, last Jewel of the valley, ass-first from her quarters and into his commander's audience.

∿

Local Walks: The Ruins. *According to local legend, the large blocks of moonstone at the far edge of the area's largest grazing meadow are from the ancient palace. The walk that takes you there from the river cuts a pleasant half-hour's time through the forest, and the grazing meadows provide a beautiful view of the Western Mountain range. Exercise caution, as at least one hiker has fallen into an ancient shaft or pit.*

Should you choose to continue your walk beyond the Ruins, terrain will shortly become rough. The Valley narrows rapidly as the foothills of the mountains encroach.

> ...*from* A Guide to the Remote River
> Valleys, *by M. Lankin, East Quadril*

∿

In the moonstone hall where generations of valley kings

had held court, Sima's robe left a muddy smear on the pale tiles. When she lifted her head, she saw Lin, draped in her chains, hauled through the broken doors behind her.

Despair, the gems said. Sima fought against the word, though it wrapped her tight.

"We caught this one over the wall," the first soldier said, pushing Sima down before the amber throne. Lin was deposited beside her a moment later. All around them, mountain army guards cleaned their swords and tipped crates of belongings onto the floor.

"These two are all who remain? Impossible. Find the lapidary." Commander Nal's voice rang sharp across the moonstones. Her soldiers rushed to obey her.

A woman at the head of an army. Sima's surprise must have registered on her face, because the soldier delivered a slap so hard it nearly sat her down on the moonstone tiles. Through blurred eyes, Sima eyed the commander's cloak, looking for the Star Cabochon. The cabochon was the largest ruby in the six kingdoms and the only one that blazed with a six-armed star. Neither Sima nor Lin had found it when they'd searched the bodies of the dead in the palace. She'd found the setting. Had known her father had broken its bindings because for one long moment the cabochon's unfettered voice had pounded her ears. She had felt its desires—the wants of the deep earth, the pressures wrought by age and power—and had almost been bent to its will. Then the voice silenced and Sima's father had plummeted from the palace wall, broken.

If the commander had the cabochon, she could compel anyone to do anything she wanted. Whole kingdoms, even.

But the commander wore a plain baldric and iron spurs, not gems. Her heels rang against moonstone when she stepped forward to inspect the platinum cuffs on Lin's wrists, the tight bands at Lin's ankles. Though her eyes looked tired and she ran a hand through her dusty hair, the commander bore the grime of a battle fought, not watched. She rode with her men, Sima realized.

Jewels did not do that. They'd needed no armies, thanks to the gems.

"The lapidary knew my terms," Commander Nal said in a voice as cold as Lin's chains. "The valley's most powerful gems for me and a royal Jewel to wed for my son. The strength of mountain and valley together will make a most powerful kingdom. But this is not a veil that will be removed easily, and there are no gems. What is this trick?"

Two guards carried the answer into the hall. A broken body, the man's ruined face turned black with blood.

At the sight, Nal stepped back. Her spurs sounded alarm.

"The gems broke your lapidary, Commander," Lin said from behind her veil of chains. "They destroy anyone who does not know how to control them." She lifted her head to meet Nal's gaze. Then her chains rang as she bowed low. "If your terms included all that remained of the valley's treasury, I present my dowry."

Sima watched Nal's eyes narrow. She'd seen that look before, on her father's face. The commander hated dissent. Or, Sima reasoned, feared it enough to destroy it. Sima wished the gems hidden in her cloak would whisper calm to Lin, to herself. Instead, the gems urged *Escape*. They would not be controlled. Sima held herself still. Focused on Lin and what she could do for her without gems.

Lapidaries heed their Jewel first, gems second. The band that had bound her left forefinger. A vow for a leader's lapidary, though Lin was raised to marry rather than rule. Her lapidary had needed the skill only to make ornaments that soothed and calmed. Sima had no experience making the glittering weapons that, with the right whisper, sang in a way that compelled those within earshot and beyond.

Lin's chains shook as she stood upright again.

Nal's advisors leaned in and murmured advice. Nal held up a hand and moved two steps closer, her boots beating back the quiet. She pulled Lin forward first, then nodded to her men. At her gesture, several guards put their hands on the grate beside the throne.

The white-jade columns of the valley's royal hall echoed with the sound of metal grinding stone as the soldiers uncovered the ancient pit again. A new, rank smell rose into the hall.

They tossed the body of the king's lapidary into the pit and left the grate open.

Lin, her golden eyes hidden behind the veil's chains, stayed silent. Resolute. As she watched, Sima vowed she would not cringe. She would not pull the stones from the cloak, though they whispered *Freedom* and *Power*.

If Nal knew what she bore in her cloak, Sima would not be Lin's lapidary for long. Whether Nal had the Star Cabochon or not.

Nal spoke so that all could hear her. "When you marry my son tomorrow, Jewel, your people will see your face filled with happiness. Then they will follow your example. Remove the veil now."

Lin swallowed. "Forgive me, Commander, but I cannot. My lapidary spoke binding charms when she soldered my veil around me. As with our mail, which you know well, these chains cannot be cut."

Nal's face flushed red and a hush passed over her soldiers. She seemed used to being obeyed.

Lapidaries must obey their Jewel. Sima clenched the

aching fingers of her right hand around her left sleeve. In her cloak, hidden gems whispered to her. *Escape.* Any gem-speaker, trained lapidary or not, in the room would hear them and know of Sima's doubts, her betrayals. Sima's shoulders bent. None heard her shame. She was indeed the last lapidary.

"And the rest of my terms. Where are they?" Nal said, so quietly that only Lin and Sima could hear. "The gems. Especially the Star Cabochon."

Sima startled. She had been so sure her father had hidden the cabochon for the commander to find or dispatched it to them after he'd pried loose the setting. How else to explain the fierce way the mountain army had followed their commander through the valley?

But the cabochon was lost to Nal as well. Sima realized she could see a crack in the commander's show of strength. She wanted power, but to hold it, she needed the gems.

Sima's own fears shook her as much as the look on Nal's face. If someone found the gem and could not bind it properly; if a wild gem-speaker came across the cabochon . . . Sima could barely stand at the thought. Only the Jewels and their lapidaries could keep the valley safe from uncontrolled gems.

But no one had thought the Jeweled Court could fall, leaving two teenage girls to fend for themselves.

No one, thought Sima, *except for the king's own lapidary, in his madness.*

"Where is it," Nal whispered again. She'd mistaken the girls' silence for collusion. "You will give it to me. You will obey me," she said to Lin. The commander's face was turning red.

Sima looked at Lin, praying she would remain silent. If they couldn't escape, perhaps they could look useless.

The guard who'd carried Sima into the hall stepped forward. He tore the gray cloak from Sima's shoulders and threw it at Nal's feet. Everyone heard the clatter that it made as the hem split and small gems spilled. The guard removed Sima's belt and took the pouch from it. Poured Sima's vows on the floor.

Nal turned her eyes to Sima, recognition in her gaze. Her voice smoothed, suddenly back in control. "And you will speak it for me, lapidary."

Defeat, whispered the gems. Sima knew she would never escape now. She would be bound again, and not to Lin.

Then Lin looked up, shards of skin and eye visible through small gaps in the chains. Her eyes spoke defiance. *Revenge.*

~

Lin hoped her voice carried clear across the court like her father's voice had. "Lapidaries are difficult to control, Commander. They are not as strong as they seem, either. Look at what happened to your traitor." She raised her eyes to meet Nal's and felt the woman's breath hot on her chains. A woman. With a son to marry. And a hunger for a kingdom of her own.

Who needed a lapidary to speak the stones for her.

While Sima stood stiff and shocked at Lin's side, Lin continued to lie. "I ordered the Star Cabochon destroyed. All you will find in that cloak are minor gems. The kind we give to children."

Speaking the words almost made them true.

Lin heard whispers behind her, the soldiers wondering at the name of the gem, at its fate. They were intrigued by their commander's demand. By the gems on the floor. She'd promised them riches. The guards sorted through the small hoard.

"Nothing shaped like a cabochon here, Commander," said the one who had carried Sima through the door.

Nal would never hold the cabochon, Lin vowed. Listening to the soldiers joke as they dragged her into the hall, she knew the Western Mountains wished to use it to enslave the valley's own people. And then they would move on to the other kingdoms.

Beside her, Sima stood steadfast in the face of Nal's

anger and Lin's own betrayal. Lin drew strength from her presence. She straightened her back. Squared her shoulders.

"You are lying," Nal said. She raised her voice so that the soldiers assembled in the moonstone court could hear. "We know your father was too weak to use your valley's gems properly, and too weak to destroy them." Nal lowered her gaze and stared down her nose at Lin. "And you are no better than your father."

What would a proper Jewel do now? Lin thought quickly. Aba's guidance was lacking here too. Lin's father would have turned his back, as he'd done when his lapidary disagreed. Lin responded with silence, lifted her chin higher. Her veil chimed with the motion.

Nal huffed softly and glared at Lin. Then, with a sweep of her cloak and her step ringing on the hall floor, the commander turned away from the Jewel and bowed to Sima.

A guard grappled Lin by her chains and dragged her to the pit. She struggled but forced her mouth shut. She would not call out. She spun in her captor's arms and looked at Sima once more. The lapidary's eyes were wide with shock.

Nal spoke in the crisp cadence of command. "Lapidary, you abandoned your vows once already today by running away. Do it again. Leave your Jewel and serve me instead." Then her voice softened. She reached out to Sima. "Your Jewel has declared you weak. I think you are strong. Cut new stones, train new lapidaries. Undo the chain bindings. Speak the gems for me. You will be well rewarded."

Lin held her breath as they lowered her into the pit, hoping to hear Sima's answer over the sound of the chains against the metal walls.

~

Under Nal's gaze, Sima began to sweat. If Nal were the ruler now, she could command a lapidary of her own. But Sima was bound to Lin. Or she had been.

Power, whispered the stones.

Sima thought of the long river and the world beyond the valley. A world she had never seen. She looked at Lin. *A lapidary protects their Jewel.*

Sima shook her head. She tried to shape her words as disappointment, not dissent. "The cutting wheels were broken before your army came, Commander. There are no more gems. And I am not a very good lapidary."

Nal narrowed her eyes. "You risk her life as well as yours."

Sima shook her head again. "To do otherwise would destroy me. As it destroyed my father." *As you destroyed him,* she thought.

Despair, whispered the small gems scattered on the floor.

Nal growled, "Find a way around your vows, or you will both die like your fathers." Her boots struck the moonstone, scratched it raw. Sima looked up in time to see a glimmer of fear behind the anger in the commander's eyes before the guards dragged Sima to the pit.

Sima recoiled at the thought of more time among the dry bones and echoes of the palace in her ears. But the guards did not hesitate as Nal looked on. They wrapped a long rope around Sima's chest. Her spine scraped the cold walls and her armpits ached as they sent her down again. Her ears rang with the sound of the grate sliding shut and locking this time. The distant echoes of Lin's weeping.

Sima's shoe brushed something soft, then slipped on a bloody robe. She stifled a cry. The morning light shone through the grate, revealing the ancient boneyard's base. Sima's foot rested on her father's robe, beside his broken body.

If she began screaming now, she thought, she might not be able to stop.

~

Lin untangled the platinum chains from around her feet and scrambled away from the soft pile of cloth she'd landed on. She smelled dried blood and fluids and, beneath it, an edge of rot. She heard a rat skitter away as a dislodged finger bone clattered to the floor.

A Jewel does not cry.

Slowly Lin moved toward a heavy body splayed on the ground. To where a bare foot held an obscene angle. The tumble had freed it from heavily embroidered purple robes and soft shoes plucked of their jewels. She rested her hand on her father's ankle, seeing it clearly: cold and stiff. Gone.

No one was coming to help, not from the Eastern Seas or any of the kingdoms. No one knew what had happened.

She bit back a sob. She could find her brothers' and sisters' bodies in the pit. She could lie down among them and die here. She could end the Jeweled Valley kingdom and thwart Nal that way.

But if she did that, the valley's people would be enslaved by the army. Forced to work the mines until Nal found more gems. If Lin lived, she might help the people, somehow. And her father had cared more about the people than anything else.

Lin tried to lift her hand, to pull away from the dead. Her body resisted. "Let me go, then," she whispered. "Let me lead them."

She found she could stand. Her chains still hung heavy on her, but as she rose away from her father's corpse, she began to think of all the lessons she'd learned hiding behind curtains and at doorways. She might not know how to fight like a Jewel, but she knew enough to form her own plan. She would need to best the Western Mountains commander.

Tomorrow Nal would force Lin to marry a child and gain herself a kingdom. She would search until the cabochon was found, then use it. Unless, Lin thought. Unless there was a way to bind Nal, to make her choose differently.

She could offer Commander Nal a different gem, dug from one of the old skulls in the pit. Or perhaps she could find a silent one, something she and Sima had missed in their previous search. She could offer that. Lie about its powers. Lin had heard such tactics discussed over the price of mail and baubles sent beyond the valley. Of prices for gemstones with the valley's mystique, but, due to cut or disposition, without their power.

If there wasn't a suitable gem, Lin thought, she could fall back on her original plan: resistance. Nal was the usurper. Lin was the Jewel. Perhaps, in time, her actions—and her horrible, hot, chafing veil—might inspire the people of the valley to rebel against their captors.

Perhaps Lin could live with that. Especially with Sima by her side. And especially if Nal did not have the Star Cabochon.

The kingdom is your setting. You are its light.

She looked at her father's waxen face then, at the long stretch of his body. It was up to her, now.

She would be the valley's Jewel, no matter the cost.

From the other side of the pit, she heard commotion. Sima scrambled against the wall as she was lowered into the pit. She had refused Nal too.

The lapidary had always been at her side. Lin breathed relief. She would remain so. Even now, as the light's angle changed and the pit grew dim and the echoes of the dead swelled in Lin's ears.

~

A lapidary protects their Jewel.

"Come away, Lin," Sima said. Her Jewel stared unblinking at her father's corpse and did not respond. Sima found a corner clear of bones and steered Lin toward it.

Commander Nal called to them from above, "Your baubles and trinkets are worthless, lapidary." A rain of the smallest lesser gems pelted Sima and hit Lin's veil with hard sounds. "None of them do anything." Opals and topaz littered the floor, kept from breaking by their settings. Sima noticed Nal had not tossed down the emeralds and sapphires.

Still, she did not respond. She did not look up.

"Next time, it won't be gems I pour through this grate. You will have better answers for me in the morning," Nal said, then walked away, her heels loud above them. Her retreat was followed by sounds of the army clearing the hall, headed for softer quarters. Then nothing beyond the whispers of topaz and opal. *Despair. Loss.*

They tugged at her mind, trying to break it. But the gems were bound, still. And Sima still had two vows. She would not let them tempt her to set them free.

"Can you hear them, Highness?" Sima asked. Lin shook her head. That was a blessing.

Sima's father's blue cloak had fallen from his body. She'd picked it up from the ground and kneaded it in her hands now. No more gems hidden in seams or pockets. Sima kept her eye on the bodies as she folded the cloak for Lin.

"We are the kingdom now," Lin whispered as the links of her platinum veil rattled against the stone walls of their prison. Then she laughed. "Nal thought we would be easy."

"The valley made chain mail and baubles, Highness. Not fighters," Sima said. "Without the great gems to protect us, Nal is right."

In the shadows that her eyes were slowly becoming accustomed to, Sima saw Lin's head dip under the weight of her veil. She knew so well the sharp angles of Lin's cheekbones, the soft curve of her ear. These were features that demanded a fine gold diadem linked to a thin nose ring, to draw the eye down to the lips. Not heavy chains.

"If I were a proper lapidary," Sima began, remembering what Lin had said to Nal.

"Your father was a proper lapidary," Lin countered, before she pressed her hands to her lips.

"He could hear gems, and control them. He mastered the art of binding; he could cut new gems. All of this made him powerful and greedy for more. But without his vows, he was no lapidary." Sima choked the words out. "As for me? I abandoned you, then failed to run away. I am no better at my vows."

Lin looked at Sima, holding her gaze. "You kept your vows. You did not betray me." She stroked Sima's hair. The platinum chains jangled as her hand moved.

With her words, the gems were silenced. Sima breathed relief. *A lapidary obeys their Jewel.*

When she was three, she'd heard the gems for the first time and her father had celebrated, showering the court with garnets and carnelian. She'd clawed her ears bloody until her father had given her the first vow. Had taken the voices away with heat and metal. "Only lapidaries can hear the gems, though all are compelled to obey. Only lapidaries can speak the gems," he'd praised her, cautiously. More bands followed against the endless barrage of whispers from the valley's gems. She'd traced her vows until her fingers ached. *A lapidary must. A lapidary must not.*

She'd learned to bind weak gems with metal bands, quieting them. She'd set them and taught them to whisper small hopes, to reflect her intent, not amplify her fears. She'd learned to draw a bead of solder along a join with heat. But the greater gems had refused to answer her or obey. Father had smoothed her hair so when she'd failed to invoke a gem, though his hands trembled. "The greater gems ignore you," he'd said, "because you fear them. You have no reason to fear them. A setting stills a gem's wildness. Your vows protect you from their whispers. With a great gem in an expert bezel, you can bind a kingdom, or destroy it."

Sima had tried harder. But when the king betrothed the youngest Jewel, the last of his children, to a son of the Eastern Seas, Sima's father smiled. "He won't send a powerful lapidary to a seaside court. There is hope for you."

Now, as her doubts flared, the opals and topaz on the pit floor muttered *Escape. Despair.*

When Lin finally laid her head on the blue cloak, Sima rose and crossed the damp pit to tend the bodies.

Soon, the king lay in as much state as Sima could give him, his arms crossed, his body wrapped in purple. The terrible burns on his mouth, Sima covered with a strip of cloth torn from her own gown. He'd choked and clawed at his throat as the burning poison concealed in his wine had ended him. Had ended the kingdom. Aqua fortis: alumen from the mountains. Used by lapidaries to separate valley diamonds from their mineral cloaks.

A lapidary must not betray their Jewel.

She turned to stand over her father's body. All angles and shards now. Her anger surged. How could he do this to the court? To her?

He'd shouted curses and horrors from the moment he'd betrayed the king and unbound the Star Cabochon, Sima realized. Shouted more as he broke the other major gems, before he let Sima and Lin out of the pit. He'd babbled the plan at them as he'd climbed the steps up the wall, words tumbling from his mouth like water over river rocks. But he hadn't made a single sound when he fell.

He, whose pride was his ability to speak. Who had screamed and struggled for control, arguing with the gems, once his vows had broken. He had fallen silent, his jaw locked tight before he died.

Sima reached her fingers out to touch her father's mouth. It was dry as paper in the damp pit. She pulled on his lip, pressing down until his jaw parted. On her father's swollen tongue, the Star Cabochon sparkled red and wild. Sima gasped and shut the dead man's mouth before the stone could whisper her mad too.

Her father's skull, Sima realized, was what held the Star Cabochon quiet now. Kept her from going mad with its demands. Her hands shook at the thought. How they needed that gem. But could she bind it? And if she did manage that, could she command it?

Sima reached into her sleeve and groaned. Her tools were in her cloak, which Nal had taken.

A lapidary is never without their tools.

She touched her father's sleeve. Felt the hidden pocket. Loosed an inner tie. His stash of files, cutters, needle pliers, the small bezel wires and the large, the tiny strike-torch—the trust of a Jeweled Valley lapidary—unrolled onto the floor.

She looked at her father's closed mouth one last time. *A lapidary obeys Jewel first, gem second.*

Then she whispered her vows over and over to deaden the voice of the ruby. She pried the gem from her father's mouth. She wrapped it as fast as her fingers would allow in a low bezel.

The six-armed star, a titanium dioxide flaw made radiant by what surrounded it, began to glow within the ruby.

It whispered *Power.* It sang *Control.* Sima's mind spun

with images of herself on the amber throne.

She worked faster, singing to drown the gem's voice. She laced thicker platinum wire to form a claw bezel. Pressed that tight over the gem. Soldered it down. The star dimmed when she wrapped the claws, six of them, over its white arms. When she finished, Sima was drenched in sweat. Her head pounded. And she held the Star Cabochon in her palm.

She raised her head to find Lin standing beside her. She hadn't heard the Jewel's chains, she'd been so focused on the gem.

"That is beautiful work," Lin said, staring at the gem and at the body of the royal lapidary. She turned and searched Sima's face. "Can you command it?"

"I don't know. I have only tried to bind it." *To quiet it.* Sima thought she saw a flicker of worry cross Lin's face. "I do not want to risk betraying you. The cabochon will ask me to, if I am not strong enough. It wants its freedom."

"I know you will not betray me now," Lin said. "But I ask one thing before you try to speak the gem." Her hands traced her veil at her brow, where she wanted the cabochon's bezel placed. "Solder the joins so that no seams exist. And bring out the lesser gems Nal threw back, too."

Sima opened her mouth to protest.

"No, Sima," Lin said quietly. She caught Sima's hands

and held them. "This is my choice. It is what I can do for my kingdom."

Sima nodded, though her heart ached. She'd keep her vow.

"Jewels belong to the valley. The gems too," Lin said gently. "Not the other way around. Nal wants the Jewel, the valley, and the gems. She wants to make her son a king. She wants the gems to control the people. I must make her choose."

A lapidary who betrays her Jewel is shattered.

Sima remembered her father's voice causing the cabochon to glow whenever he'd said its name. Such control. Such power. Soon it had glowed all the time. She remembered how her father had sent to the mountains for supplies he needed to cut new stones to strengthen the kingdom. Aqua fortis, muriatic.

"We must use the cabochon against Nal first. To compel her to leave." *A lapidary must.* Sima swallowed her fear and gathered the lesser gems from the pit floor, sparkling in their bezels. She sparked the torch and began to solder the chains around the Star Cabochon's bezel. The veil, which had hung loose, pulled taut against Lin's back and neck. "Is it too much?" she asked.

"Keep going."

Sima placed the lesser gems in the chains of Lin's veil, wherever they fit. She invoked them as best she could.

When moonlight sifted through the grate, the set gems whispered: opals spoke of *rebellion;* the topaz of *revenge.* Only the Star Cabochon was silent.

"This could doom you," she whispered to Lin.

"You are not your father. No hidden faults. No secret temptations. The gems bent him, and the mountains too."

Sima nodded, hoping Lin was right. She set a final stone in Lin's cuff.

Lin watched and mused, "Would you help me now if you weren't oath-bound to me?"

Her words hung in the dark air. Sima remembered the crunch of gravel beneath her feet, the sound of the distant river beyond the burning village. Her hands smoothed the chains on Lin's veil. Her fingers counted the stones: an opal from Lin's mother's ring; a blue topaz from Lin's brother's sword, chipped and bloodied.

No greater honor in the valley than to have the gems speak to you, Sima remembered. The greater the gem, the greater the honor. The greater the risk. The engraved bands said so. Father too.

"I will not leave you again," Sima vowed. "My birth binds me, as does yours."

As she said it, she felt the strength of this vow in her bones. All the gems fell silent.

"Will you attempt speaking the cabochon?" Lin

asked, kneeling so that Sima's mouth was close to the ruby's curved dome.

Sima moistened her lips. If Lin asked it, she would.

"Star Cabochon," Sima whispered, "bound by your bezel, obey." Her words sank into the ruby and pulled her breath with it. The star pulsed once in the dark and her heart quickened. "Obey," she repeated, focusing harder than ever before, though her voice faded. The ruby stole her breath but remained silent.

Sima coughed and gagged. She was not strong enough.

Lin sank to the damp ground to comfort her attendant. "You help me in other ways." She sounded so tired.

Of course, thought Sima. *A lapidary must.* Sima spoke the gems she could: Breathed on two opals set at Lin's ears: *Rest;* Whispered the perfectly faceted topaz she'd cut herself: *Peace.*

As she did so, Sima wished for a gem that could stop time. Or one that would bring back the dead. What facets would need to be cut to return the Jeweled Court? She had charms against fear, but nothing more potent. She was worse than useless if she could not protect them both from the morning.

Lin calmed. "You are so good with the pleasant gems," she murmured. "Tomorrow, Sima, we will see what they choose."

A lapidary obeys her Jewel. Sima bit back a sob. Fear. And loss. She didn't need gems to amplify those. She concealed her tools in her sleeve and let Lin lean against her, pressing the chains between them into her skin.

~

Local Walks: The Jeweled Valley Artisans. *As cottage-crafts have again become fashionable, a valley visitor may ask at the Band and Chain for directions to local artisans. The region has few options as compared to other towns mentioned in this guide. However, traditional jewelers still practice local methods for setting semiprecious and precious stones, from wrapping to bezel-setting. When offered the opportunity to purchase a real Jeweled Valley gemstone, note that chips and shards made available to visitors are, at best, of ill quality and, at worst, colored glass. Inquiring after gemstones that sing or speak will not endear you to the local population.*

> . . . *from* **A Guide to the Remote River Valleys,** *by M. Lankin, East Quadril*

~

When she woke, Lin lay still, so Sima would think she still dreamed. Her lapidary could not protect her from

The Jewel and Her Lapidary

dreams, she knew. She shrugged off the dark gauze of her nightmare: her brothers and sisters, kissing her on her wedding day and then turning to ash.

A Jewel must put kingdom first and self second. This is what Aba should have told her. Instead Aba whispered about beautiful children and fine palaces. About *duty* and *grace*. About *love*. Lin, for her part, had dreamed of seeing the Eastern Seas. She'd looked forward to knowing the world beyond the valley. She had hoped she would grow to love her betrothed and his people.

The gaze of her own valley people had terrified her when she first went through the streets with her father. Behind her veil, she felt their eyes desperate for a glimpse of more than her profile. Their hopes for her sat heavy on her brow. She'd recoiled, and her father had noticed.

A people's love is not an easy thing. You must return it in kind or it will devour you.

A lapidary's love too. For there was Sima, always watching her. Finding new ways to protect her, to soothe her.

Lin thought how her fingers might feel unencumbered by baubles. Her brow unmarred by a crown. How she might pass through the streets unrecognized, without her lapidary by her side.

If she could have laughed now, without rousing Sima, she would have.

From the corner of her slitted eyes Lin saw her father's feet covered in a purple robe. Sima thought her too delicate to tend her own father.

Well. Weren't most Jewels too delicate? Relying on gems for their influence. Making gems that kept the valley from danger instead of confronting it. Her father had allowed the royal lapidary almost every duty, from assigning courtiers to the design and purpose of new gems. Even the selection of diplomats and traders to negotiate prices on valley goods had been left to lapidaries. Father was interested in the well-being of the people, nothing more. He loved them. And the people loved him for it.

But when Lin peeked through a part in the royal hall's tapestries, she could see the royal lapidary looking at her father as if he were a prize gem, shaped and bound.

What had Aba said about the lapidaries? That they'd once sat on the amber throne, in the days when the gems ruled the valley. Lin didn't want to believe that. She saw how they bound themselves in their vows to keep the gems' voices at bay. How they stood between the Jewels and their gems, controlling them and controlled by them, so that the Jewels could rule without damaging their own minds.

So much sacrifice. For what?

She felt Sima's arm press against her side as the lapidary dreamed.

When she'd asked Aba, *What would set the lapidaries free?* Aba had distracted her with a lesson on gem properties. Then she'd gone to have a talk with the king.

Lin had formed a theory. She'd heard enough whispers when she was listening behind curtains. There was one thing that would free the lapidaries and the people. Now it would thwart Nal too. The gem mines must be destroyed. Without the mines, the existing gems would grow old and eventually chip or break. Some in the valley might hear raw gems, but those, still set deep in the earth, wouldn't strain to compel a person to their will. They wouldn't need to be controlled. So many of the great gems, the ones that had caused all the problems in the past, were now destroyed. Except for the cabochon.

Perhaps, Lin thought, the gem veins underground had waned. It was true that few powerful gems had been found in recent years. Few that could be cut and bound, fewer still that would bring great power to a dangerous person. She'd overheard her father's lapidary wanting to arm the valley, to consolidate power; her father had muttered something and stormed out. The lapidary had paced, trapped.

If the mines were shut, eventually the voices would quiet and the lapidaries would be free.

At least one would.

The valley would have to learn to stand on its own.

What would Sima choose? Lin wondered. If she could speak the powerful gems and control them as her father had? Would she choose never to hear them again?

The thought made Lin afraid for herself, a little.

What would Nal choose if she gained the power of the gems? If she gained a lapidary of her own? Lin shuddered and vowed the valley would never find out.

Lin slowly sat up, and Sima woke. The two stared at each other silently. Then Sima sat up too. "I don't want you to suffer, Lin," she said. Lin heard the tremble in her voice and felt a lump in her throat. They were two alone, against an army.

Before that horrible night, Sima had slept at her bedside. Tended her every need. She was still tending Lin, trying to fulfill her vows. Lin searched for a way to reply, words that would mean something. "I want you to be free," she finally said. "Of the gems. Of the Jewels."

Sima's face folded in confusion. "That is not my path. We are joined."

"You've never wanted more?"

Her lapidary was silent. Of course she had. Everyone wanted more. Even Lin. She'd wanted to see the Eastern Seas. To remove her veil in public. To fall in love.

Jewels didn't fall in love. Aba had said so.

Long ago, Lin had seen one of her brothers with his lapidary. She'd known from the way their eyes did not meet that there was no love when they kissed. That what passed between them was just a service. Another bauble.

Lin had wondered what it would be like. Maybe not with Sima, but with someone. Her chain-veil pressed cold against her cheeks. "Would you marry?"

"I might." Sima's voice was a whisper.

"Who?"

In the past, when Sima shrugged, her vows had clattered and chimed softly. A merry sound, a bit like laughter. Now, her gesture was silent. She clasped Lin's hand and the chains around it. "I am bound, like the gems." She leaned against Lin's shoulder. Pressed her lips against the veil and Lin's cheek beneath. "Do not dwell on it, my Jewel."

Lin felt the warmth of Sima's mouth on her skin through the chill metal chains. Then Sima gasped and grabbed her head with both hands.

"My Jewel!" she whispered. "I overstepped." Her eyes darted this way and that, as if she listened to something poisonous. The lesser gems?

Lin couldn't hear them, but she knew the signs.

"I liked it," she said, taking Sima's other hand. "It's all right."

Sima blinked. She breathed calmer. Lin felt a twinge of surprise. She'd settled the gems with her own reassurances.

They sat holding hands for a long time.

The first morning light angled into the pit and gilded the edges of the bone pile. A guard climbed down a rope ladder. He gestured to them, and they stood up together. Walked side by side toward the ladder.

~

Carefully, so as to keep from tripping on her chains, Lin climbed from the pit first. Her veil chimed with each step. Her gems, even those crusted with gore, sparkled in the morning light. Sima followed her, silent. When Lin halted before the amber throne, Sima stopped too. She turned to look at the new court of the Western Mountains commander. They'd been assembled behind a wall of ironclad soldiers, many among them familiar townspeople. Heads bobbed and whispers filled the room when people saw what sat upon the Jewel's brow.

Sima tried to put her failures in the pit, as far from her thoughts as the gems' whispers.

Lin kept her eyes focused on the amber throne and Commander Nal, who now sat upon it, talking to a young boy beside her. He looked so like Nal, Sima did not doubt this was her son.

"For the last time, Jewel Lin, remove that veil so that I may present your betrothed, my son Remir." Commander Nal did not rise from the throne. She barely looked at Lin, at first. Then her gaze caught on the cabochon.

For once, Nal was speechless. She stared. Sima caught a glint of something beneath the anger. Fear. Then the commander ground her heel into the floor. "You dare to flaunt that ruby? After denying you had it." Her fingers curled around the throne's arm as if she wished to pluck the Star Cabochon from Lin's forehead like a fruit.

Meantime, the boy stared at Lin, dazzled. He could not have been more than twelve years old. Sima held her breath.

"Once again, Commander, I cannot remove the veil." Lin's cloaked face gave nothing away.

Sima let her breath out and whispered to the Star Cabochon: *Compel them to leave.* The six-arm star glowed deep inside the ruby's polished dome and made no reply. Sima felt defeat tear at her throat once more.

A lapidary must know her limits when invoking the gems of the court.

Lin turned her head left, then right, acknowledging the valley artisans gathered beyond the rows of guards. The tiny chains of her garment rang softly as she turned again. She paused when her eyes reached Remir.

So young, Sima thought. *He will not lead. His mother will.*

The boy, clothed in bleached goat leather, stared at

Lin's golden skin, barely visible between the platinum links and gemstones that wrapped her from head to ankle. He cleared his throat. When he spoke, his voice pitched high and cracked. "Why can't you?"

Nal turned to address her son, but Lin spoke first.

"My father did not need the Star Cabochon to command our people. He had their love. You have tried to take the valley by stealth and force. And now by marriage. So you must choose: the Star Cabochon, or me."

Lin lifted her arms, and chains ran like silver rivers up her arms to the thick bezel at her brow. "My lapidary spoke shatter charms. Breaking the chains will destroy the cabochon. You are right that we cannot do it ourselves, but you can."

Remir's mouth opened. He cocked his head, listening. Lin's chains jangled, the only sound in the hall. Then the meaning of Lin's words swept across the moonstone tiles, around the white-jade pillars. Sima heard stifled gasps. Guards in battle-scarred mail gripped the hilts of their swords.

But it was Remir's reaction that was most interesting to Sima. He swayed before the Star Cabochon. And the star glowed in return. Unless Sima was seeing things.

Sima felt her heart race. Perhaps Remir could hear gems. Perhaps he could hear a stone that she could not. With no training. And no vows.

Lapidaries must train all those who hear the stones.

The engraved bands demanded this duty of all lapidaries. Could Sima manage it where she had failed in so many things? Sima jumped, startled from her thoughts when Nal's fist slammed against the amber throne.

"When we made our offer, Jewel Lin, it was in good faith. You present us with a false promise of your own."

Lin did not answer. She did not look up. Days ago, she would have cried in fear or looked to her brothers for help. She had already learned more than a youngest Jewel should ever know. *An opaque diplomacy,* Sima thought. *While I have gained little skill with the Star Cabochon.*

Remir turned to Sima, his voice clear and high. "You made these chains. You can undo it. Set her free."

A lapidary who betrays their Jewel is shattered.

Sima's fingers flexed. She willed them still. That was not Lin's command. Sima would be no better than her father if she betrayed her Jewel.

The doors to the royal hall—now reinforced with iron—creaked open. Across the hall, ten guards pushed an enormous rock crystal vase. Mountain ranges and a river valley had been carved into the vase's sides. Metal wheels rattled over the moonstone tiles, groaning under the weight of the vase. When the guards stopped before the amber throne, the wheels squeaked and the crystal resonated with a high-pitched tone.

"Your wedding gift, Jewel Lin," Nal said. She held out a hand to her son, who looked at the vase, then back to Lin, his eyes wide. Nal's dark gaze took in the assembled court. "Do you not see the Western Mountains' wealth and strength?"

The vase towered over Lin and Sima. Its value was beyond measure.

Lin, in a clear voice, said, "The valley's strength is its people, Commander. Not in gems or armor."

Nal tutted. "Surely you've learned from your father's example, Jewel Lin?"

Sima shivered at the memory of the bodies in the pit and the night spent watching over their broken bones.

The commander drew a deep breath. "We need the valley, its artisans and miners, its mail. The armies of the east threaten us even now." Her eyes hardened to two dark stones. She pressed her lips together. "There is one way through. We have brought with us more aqua fortis for refining gems and metal. We have muriatic from our iron and salt mines."

Nal turned to Sima. "Do you know what happens when you combine muriatic and aqua fortis, lapidary?"

"Aqua regia." *Water of kings.* The words escaped Sima's mouth before she could seal her lips. She'd used the combination once under her father's instruction to dissolve a gold setting from around a stone. Later she'd poured off the gold and recaptured it. But not before she'd burned skin from her arm with the acid. She swallowed, remembering. Lin's veil made a shifting sound, but the Jewel did not speak.

Remir paled. "You wouldn't. Can't you hear them?"

His mother ignored him. *She should be careful,* Sima thought.

But then Nal ordered Sima, "You will cut her out of this and in no way damage the Star Cabochon. What happens to the Jewel is of waning interest to me."

Her son opened his mouth to argue, but Nal stopped him with her hand. "We will not be held hostage by our conquests and their archaic rules," she said. "We have our own people to protect."

She waved forward a guard, bearing the bulky tools of a Mountain mine. The guard pressed a cold iron saw into Sima's hand.

The vase loomed before Sima, hard and clear. The court of her ancestors stood silent. She remembered the burn of aqua regia on her arm and weighed her vows to Lin. *Betrayal,* whispered a topaz in Lin's veil.

She startled when Lin's fingers grazed her free hand. Then a sharp point poked her right index finger. The culet of a gem, pressed from Lin's fingers to hers: a blue topaz. The gem whispered *Courage.*

Sima took a deep breath and in her steadiest voice

spoke the words that Lin demanded of her. "Commander, I cannot."

At their commander's gesture, three guards brought a wooden ladder and half-hauled, half-lifted Lin into the vase. Then Sima. The iron tools they took away.

When they were finished, Nal stood and pointed to the vase. "Tomorrow, we will fill that vase with aqua regia. The gems and platinum she wears will be ours, and we will have no need of a burial. Your people will have nothing left to love." Nal pushed her son from the room, calling over her shoulder, "I suggest you remember a way to free her first."

The court grew noisy with shouts as the soldiers cleared the room. "The Jewel of the people," someone cried before an ironclad guard struck him down and dragged him away.

The moonstone tiles rang with metal striking metal as the remaining guards threw newly wrought iron bolts across the court's doors.

∼

Lin leaned against Sima inside the echoing vase. She had no words to describe the sadness she felt. Aba hadn't taught her anything near enough to face this. The hall reverberated with her kingdom's losses.

The walls of the vase showed the valley in reverse, the mountains and clouds clear cuts in the crystal, while the sky was opaque. The cold of the crystal made her chains freeze. The Star Cabochon felt heavy on Lin's brow. She tried to think.

Nal's goal was legitimacy. A kingdom of her own. Lin wondered what Nal's doubts were. What could make her loose her grasp on the valley long enough for the people to rebel? She'd seen something when she'd said "no" to Nal. Not only strength. Fear too.

Nal had expected to find a lapidary she could control. She'd planned treachery, not a battle of wills. With either of them.

Lin turned to look at Sima. Her lapidary's face was more familiar than her own. Always by her side. Sima's golden skin and dark eyes were faded with exhaustion and hunger. She suffered. Lin wished she could ease Sima's pain. But she could neither speak the gems nor hear them. She was glad for that. Gems could be stolen or broken. They could be turned against you. To rely on them was to become weak. That had been her father's mistake. And it was about to be Nal's.

But Sima's loyalty had proven stronger than both gems and fear. Lin felt her friend's strength shore up her own reserves. She needed the lapidary as much as her father had needed the gems.

To face down Nal and deny her commands, Lin needed all of her strength. With a start, Lin realized that Sima was prepared to remain with her, no matter what happened. She would die at Lin's side.

"*No,*" Lin whispered. There had to be another way. She would not ask the lapidary to die for her. If that weakened her as a Jewel, so be it.

But would Sima risk escape again, if she ordered her to? What would distract the guards? If she could escape, would Sima be strong enough to take Lin's message to the valley people? That the mines must be destroyed? The supports pulled from the caverns and holes dug to let in river and rain until the shafts collapsed? If Sima could find enough alum and aqua fortis—and here Lin felt a slightly hysterical laugh rise in her chest like a bubble—the valley's farmers could combine that with guano and fertilizer to blow up the mines too.

So many things she wanted to tell her people. Lin hoped Sima would be able to make them listen. She hoped her own sacrifice would be enough of a message to them.

Sima's eyes were dark as bloodstone as she searched Lin's visage. For once, Lin was glad of the veil. She kept silent and watched her friend, holding her face in her memory. Feeling the kiss on her cheek again.

Sima opened her mouth to speak, but Lin pressed a

finger against her lips. She'd made her choice. Sima could not protect her from what she would do.

~

Lapidaries must never be without their tools.

Sima stared at Lin through the chains. Lin's finger rested for a long time on her lips, and Sima did not brush it away. When the moon rose and light streamed through the high windows set in the palace walls, the moonstone tiles and white-jade columns glowed.

She counted the guards. Wished she could speak a gem to make them lean on their weapons and sleep. No. She could only make Lin sleep. Worse than worthless here.

"I am sorry," Lin said. "I would release you from your vows." Her chains screeched against the rock crystal.

The gems fell silent. Sima's jaw worked. *Freedom. Escape. Betrayal.*

Finally she spoke. "You are protecting our people." Sima was embarrassed that her voice broke. She still lacked strength. "You are my Jewel. I will not leave you."

The last Jewel, Sima thought. *My Lin. A lapidary must protect their Jewel. A lapidary must obey their Jewel.* The two vows, still wrapping her earlobes, fought each other in Sima's mind. No one in the Jeweled Valley Court could have predicted that. So many vows had been broken already. The gems sensed her struggle. They reached for her weaknesses, hoping to amplify them. Sima pressed her hands to her ears at their whispers. Breaking more vows would destroy her and Lin too. Not breaking them would have the same effect. She had to choose.

Sima reached inside her sleeve for her tools. *Bravery,* sang the blue topaz Lin had given her, tucked into Sima's left vow. *Calm,* said the opals at Lin's ears. Sima looked at the chains, where she'd made the solders and joins.

In the silence of the evening, she heard another sound, from the left of the throne. The guards' door opening. Footsteps.

"Step outside," a young voice ordered. Iron armor screeched and a man laughed. The guards stayed where they were. "I would speak to my betrothed alone," the voice said again. "Commander Nal said I should try to reason with her."

At this, the guards grumbled but agreed to step outside the great doors. The hall rumbled with their movements, then stilled.

A face pressed against the side of the vase. Remir. Lin's intended. Sima nudged Lin and pointed.

"The gem said I should come," Remir stuttered. His words came muffled through the glass. His face was a blur, but first one hand, then the other pressed against the glass. "Earlier. But I couldn't get away."

Which gem? Sima wondered. "Can you hear them now?" *How could he hear them, when Lin could not?*

Remir's hands slid down the vase. "Only sometimes. Faint. Not now. I can get you out. I have a rope."

"What does he mean, Sima?" Lin whispered low enough that Remir didn't hear her.

Sima chewed her lip. Another gem-speaker? Untrained. And old enough that he might be dangerous. "Why risk your mother's anger just because you think you heard something?"

Remir stepped back. "I did hear it. And now I want to help you. My mother is going about this the wrong way."

"She didn't send you here tonight," Lin said.

"No."

Sima's thoughts raced. Perhaps they did not need to escape. Perhaps the valley's legacy was not lost. If Lin and Remir married and Sima trained Remir, the valley might someday regain power within the Mountain kingdom. She pictured herself wrapping Remir's arms with metal bands. She wondered if he was too old to learn the vows. If he would one day break, like the King's Lapidary.

She wondered what the boy would choose, if he could: gems or people.

His face once again pressed against the glass, as close to Lin and the gems as he could get.

"Would you support me against Nal, Remir? Would you choose me over the gems?" Lin asked. She had the same questions as Sima. Her voice filled with hope.

The blur of Remir's head nodded. "I would."

But Sima noticed his hesitation. The crack in his voice. A flaw? Perhaps. Or a lie.

"We could slip away tonight," Remir continued. "The guards would chase us, but we could use the gem against them. It told me so."

He would use a gem against his own people. The cabochon. *It told me so.* More than a flaw. Sima reached for Lin's hand. She thought of Lin's vision: the valley safe from conquerors and cabochon. Sima thought quickly. The gems. The topaz and opals she knew she could command. *Calm. Forget.* If Remir heard the cabochon through the wall of the vase, perhaps the others could reach him too.

For a moment, the cabochon's star glowed unbidden at Lin's forehead, then faded.

"I won't allow the Star Cabochon to survive," Lin said. "If I cannot break it, I will bury it."

"I understand," Remir said. "I will help you." His voice was oddly flat.

Sima realized she was shaking her head slowly from side to side. This felt wrong. Remir was too willing to agree. "Prove it," she said. "Tomorrow. Argue Lin's case before the court. Before Nal. Protect the Jewel."

"Is that your wish, Lin?" The boy's voice was calm, though the vase made it echo strangely. He waited. Sima began to whisper.

"It is," Lin said.

"Remir, listen," Sima said. *Sleep,* she whispered to the opals. *Walk away,* to the topaz.

Remir yawned. His hands pulled away from the crystal wall of the vase. Lin and Sima listened to his footsteps recede. The guards' door opened, then closed.

"Perhaps we have a chance," Lin whispered, uncertain. She yawned too.

Sima was not so sure. "The boy," she said, "can hear the gems. The Star Cabochon."

Lin's grip on Sima's hand tightened, but Sima was staring at the gem on her brow. When she spoke its name, it had glowed. It had heard her. It hadn't answered, but that was a start. A better chance.

Sima slowly turned, scraping an arm against the rough crystal. Her eyes searched for Lin's through the veil of chains. The room had darkened with moonset. The thought of what the dawn would bring, of the aqua regia's acrid smell filling the room, the orange gas bubbling, and the screams, made Sima speak quickly. "The gem controls him, as his mother does. He is untrained. You would not survive long here. You must escape." *Escape.*

"You could fix it, Sima," Lin said. "You spoke the gem just now. The look on your face gave you away."

"Perhaps," Sima answered. She imagined compelling Nal to return to the Western Mountains, teaching Remir the ways of a lapidary. She wondered if she could.

A lapidary must—

Sima thought of all the vows her father had broken; how he betrayed the valley and his Jewel. How the Mountain Court had bent his oaths.

Sima smoothed her hand across Lin's chains and whispered to the lesser gems. Lin leaned against the vase's side and touched Sima's cheek with her free hand. Sima looked at the Star Cabochon in its clutch setting. She might use it to control a future king.

A lapidary must not—

Sima couldn't breathe in the vase's confines. She gestured for Lin to move closer to her, and the exhausted Jewel obeyed. The two pressed together while Sima whispered the stones she knew well, the ones that would answer her when she kept her vows: the opals, the topaz. *Rest.*

"Sima, no," Lin murmured, but in a few minutes she slept, leaning heavily against Sima's shoulder.

Sima ran her fingers along the platinum chains and found the few rings she knew to be weakest: rings not tied to the cabochon bezel's tension setting. These she chiseled with her file. She braced Lin's forehead against her shoulder. Lin slept on.

They could both run, without Remir. The guards had not returned from their post outside the doors. She'd heard loud snoring from beyond the vase.

They could leave the chains and help each other out of the vase. They could scale the palace walls and run for the river. But the cabochon would shatter.

Lapidaries must preserve their Jewels. Lapidaries must protect the gems in their care.

Too many vows had been broken already. The loosed gems would tear Sima's mind to shreds.

Meanwhile, Nal's army would pursue Lin. Remir might learn to invoke the gems without rules or bindings. He might make more. This would drive him mad, but the destruction he might cause in the meantime made Sima work even faster. His connection to the gems would outweigh any feeling he had for the people.

Sima slid an arm into the veil, fingers spread wide to brace the chains near the bezel. She hummed to quiet the shatter charms and steadied the most important links with her files, bracing them against solder points and knots. She pushed her foot behind Lin's, then slipped three small gems from their settings. Even the Jewel didn't know about these. Lin's cuffs loosened.

Gems began to whisper as their settings were disturbed. *Revenge. Peace. Power. Sorrow. Escape.* Sima knew what they offered her. She moved faster to finish what she'd begun.

Gingerly, Sima pulled Lin, still sleeping, from the veil with one hand, while her other arm shook with the effort of bracing the headdress. Her elbow banged the vase's wall. Her head pulsed with the gems' demands. Then Sima stepped beneath the veil and lowered the headdress onto her own forehead. The chain mail and the heavy cabochon masked her face. Dear Valley, the weight.

A lapidary must work through pain.

Lin woke when the veil's burden lifted from her skin. Still groggy, she reached to pull Sima from the garment.

"We'll take the veil to the caves and hide," she said. "We will find a way."

"You must leave the cabochon here, and me with it, Lin," Sima said. "They will think the lapidary ran away again, not the Jewel. They do not know your face. They will not seek you out."

"I will no longer be a Jewel." Lin's mouth curved into a frown. The gems were silent. The white-jade columns tinted pink with the sunrise.

Sima encouraged her. "You will strengthen your people. You will lead them."

Lin looked at Sima and began to object. Sima interrupted. "This is my choice. Let me make it."

Lin nodded, her eyes soft. "To be a lapidary is a greater honor."

The gems stayed silent.

Sima gave Lin the soft blue dress she'd worn for days. It smelled rank, even from a distance. She removed the torch and the solder wire from the sleeve and began to close the chains in the mail, to tighten the cuffs around her arms. She passed Lin her files and the blue topaz. *Courage.*

Lin pushed it back. "This gem is yours."

Sima swallowed and tightened her fingers around the topaz, then pressed it into a loop of mail near her ear. She passed Lin her cloak and soldered the final loops in the veil. She invoked the gems she'd tucked in Lin's pocket: the rose topaz for peace, a king's battle opal for vengeance. Through the chains, Sima glimpsed Lin's face shining with tears.

Lin adjusted the veil so the bezel rested comfortably against Sima's forehead. She tucked Sima's tools into a sleeve.

"Go," Sima ordered her. She cupped her hands and Lin placed one foot in them. Sima lifted Lin high enough to grip the vase's edge. She listened as Lin's footsteps receded toward the guards' door, hoping that Remir had left it unbolted.

Forget, she'd whispered to him through the gems.

~

Local Walks: The Jewel and Her Lapidary. *A walk to be taken in conjunction with the Variegated Riverbank (p. 29). A half-mile downriver from the Deaf King, near the entrance to the area's largest cave, stands a limestone and cobalt formation resembling two joined figures. No more than a meter in height, the formation is said to bring luck and good fortune. According to local guides, a lapidary assigned to each member of the royal family from birth acted as advisor, servant, and jeweler. This is likely a conflation of multiple roles. Other nearby formations include the Iron Gauntlet and the Bezel.*

. . . *from* A Guide to the Remote River Valleys, *by M. Lankin, East Quadril*

~

Beyond the wall, the valley slept. A white wisp of smoke rose from a riverman's cottage in the predawn. Lin crept between the forest's shadows through the night. The snores of the Mountain guards told her no one saw her passage.

She felt the jewels impelling her onward, to escape, to regain the kingdom. She wondered at what they were saying to cause her so much confidence.

And she felt something else too. Her feet through Sima's soft shoes, stepping rough across the forest floor and its pointed leaves and nettles. Her heart, urging her into the unknown. Out of the formal setting where Lin had spent her life. She did not know how she would be received anywhere. Or if. She might be caught as a thief or a rogue. Without her robes and finery, she looked like any other young woman. She looked like Sima.

Lin clutched her fist around the gems hidden in the sleeve of her—Sima's—robe. Her eyes burned and her stomach clenched. Sima.

What had Aba told her? What had her sisters said? *To be a Jewel is a sacrifice of the heart. You must become hardened to the losses.*

She didn't want to become hard. But the valley needed a leader who understood the dangers. There was still danger, from the mountain army and from the valley's gems—the unmined stones still called from the caverns to some, they caused too much trouble when freed for those who didn't understand how to control them. Lin would have to devise ways to close the mines, to keep them hidden from the army.

Lin stumbled toward the cottage. She wrapped herself in her cloak and knelt by the small rabbit hutch, until the riverman's wife nearly tripped over her.

"Who is this?" the riverman's wife said.

~

Sunlight poured in the high windows, making the hall and the assembled court sparkle. Commander Nal addressed the valley's sole Jewel. "See how your people betray you. They do not love you after all. You will die alone. Your gems will fall into our hands, unencumbered."

Now came the hardest decision.

Sima said nothing, so her voice could not give Lin away. She did not smile, though no one would see her if she did. *A lapidary must remain resolute at all times.*

Nal's guards lifted a vat of clear muriatic to one side of the vase and a vat of clear aqua fortis to the other. The smell burned Sima's nose.

"This is your final chance, Jewel."

Sima heard Remir rise to his feet. She held her breath. She could not put him to sleep now. What would he choose?

"Please," begged the boy. Sima thought of the words she'd once worn, of teaching Remir to solder, to bind gems with metal. "Please," the boy said again. "Do what you need to, but get the gems."

Sima pressed her lips together.

Using iron grapples, the guards poured the vats' contents into the vase. The combined acids turned orange as they merged at Sima's feet. A cloud of acrid gas rose and burned her eyes. Beyond the vase's walls, she heard scrambling. Someone retched.

Sima bit her lip, vowing to stay silent as the Jeweled Valley at dawn. The burn on her arm pulsed with remembered pain. Aqua regia sluiced over the platinum chains. A small gem fell from its setting and clinked to the vase's base. Lin's older sister's rare green topaz: love. An opal: truth. Sima's eyes could not see it in the cloud. She could hear them singing. Her legs began to buckle. The pain turned her jaw to amber, her ears to opal. The topaz pulsed in her hand as the reign of the valley Jewels ended.

When Sima could bear no more, she snapped the chain mail link she'd filed nearly in half the night before. She felt a crack against her forehead.

Remir shrieked. The edge of his voice softened to a wordless howl.

Yes, whispered Sima and the gem together. *Go*, Sima whispered. *Freedom*, said the gem. *Yes*.

With a noise like a mineshaft collapsing, a scream, and a fire all at once, the Star Cabochon of the Jeweled Valley shattered in its cage.

~

"Who are you?" the riverman's wife repeated, her voice breaking on the last word. She reached for a thick piece of wood. Behind her, the boats still burned.

"Malin," the girl said, the name gem-hard in her mouth. But her heart softened with each syllable. She would carry both their memories, beyond the castle wall.

The riverman's wife held out a cautious hand, taking in Malin's courtier clothing. "You are from the palace." It was not a question.

"Not anymore." Malin took the woman's hand and walked toward the river with her.

Each step farther from the palace echoed with memories and loss. The Jewels. The gems. Sima. The sun rose and they heard a sharp sound, distant and muted. A shattering sound. She bit hard on her lip. Forced herself to stay strong.

Malin let the woman lead her past the burning boats, to a cave mouth where locals once gathered beside a small stone formation. Malin ate a few bites of food with the woman, though it tasted like ash in her mouth. Once night fell, valley men and women joined them. They asked her of news from the palace. She looked at their faces, their bruises and wounds. "The palace is lost. The

Jewels are lost."

She let them weep. Held her own tears back, still, though she was desperate to mourn. That would come later. After the valley was safe. When the people had quieted, she prepared to speak. "Before she died, the last Jewel said we must shut the mines." She let her words sink in. "We must begin to break the Mountain's grip, and the gems' hold on us, from within."

The men and women who were left of her people began to make plans, their eyes as sharp and shining as gemstones: blue and gold and deepest amber. Malin let them speak to her.

Acknowledgments

Many thanks to Tor.com for giving this book its proper setting. To my editor, Patrick Nielsen Hayden, and to Irene Gallo, for their vision; to Lee Harris, Mordicai Knode, Tommy Arnold, Christine Foltzer, Carl Engle-Laird, and Lauren Hougen.

To Paul Race and to Chris Wagner, who let me mess about with metals, stones, and oxygen-acetylene torches. To Tom Wilde, who won't let me have an oxygen-acetylene torch in the house but who answers any chemistry question put to him and only then asks, "Why do you want to know?"

To E. Catherine Tobler, Kelly Lagor, Nicole Feldringer, Chris Gerwel, Lauren Teffeau, Alex Shvartsman, Siobhan Carroll, Rachel Winchester, and A. C. Wise, who were all very patient with facets of this story.

To anyone who dreams about the layered histories of a familiar place, or an unfamiliar one, this is for you.

About the Author

Photograph by Dan Magus

FRAN WILDE's acclaimed short stories have appeared in *Asimov's Science Fiction and Fact, Beneath Ceaseless Skies, Nature,* and *Tor.com.* Her first novel, *Updraft,* debuted from Tor in 2015. She's worked as a science and engineering writer, as a programmer and game developer, as a sailing instructor, and as a jeweler's assistant. She writes about technology, culture, family, and reading for *Geek-Mom, The Washington Post,* and *SF Signal;* she blogs and podcasts about the intersection of food and fiction for *Cooking the Books* at franwilde.net. Wilde lives in Pennsylvania with her family.

TOR·COM

Science fiction. Fantasy. The universe.

And related subjects.

*

More than just a publisher's website, *Tor.com*
is a venue for **original fiction, comics,** and
discussion of the entire field of SF and fantasy,
in all media and from all sources. Visit our site
today—and join the conversation yourself.

CPSIA information can be obtained
at www.ICGtesting.com
Printed in the USA
LVOW12s1723020317
525947LV00004B/755/P